Top 10 Ways to Kill Your Boss

By
Steve Hudgins

Copyright © 2020 Steve Hudgins
All rights reserved

CHAPTER 1

Shall we begin?

So you want to kill your boss, huh?

Okay, let's get right into it. First of all you're going to need a…

Wait a minute…

I have this sneaking suspicion that your boss saw this book sitting by your desk, or station or wherever the hell you work and they picked it up. Which means…they're reading this right now!

Uh oh.

This is not good. Now they know that you want to kill them!

While the thought of murdering one's boss may flash through the mind of many employees, most sane people won't act on that demented impulse.

You on the other hand took the next step. You bought a book to find out the top 10 ways to kill your boss…and now your boss knows all about it!

I'm not a brain surgeon, but I'm pretty sure this kind of thing may be frowned upon. It probably won't reflect well on your next performance review and it may even be grounds for immediate dismissal!

That is, IF (notice how big that if is?) IF you are actually plotting to kill your boss, which of course you aren't because this is a…uh…joke! Yeah, that's right. This is nothing more than a fun loving innocent joke intended to make people laugh and nothing more!

Haha! So what do you think, boss? Isn't this funny?
Wow! The expression on your face!
That was a good one huh?
What a sense of humor your wonderful employee has!
There's nothing like a great sense of humor to boost morale at the workplace, that's for sure.
Hell, I think this jolly employee deserves a raise, don't you?

LOL!

Well, that was quite the laugh. Okay, now that you know this was just a gag, you can go ahead and put this book down.

I hope you enjoyed the fun. Have a pleasant remainder of your day.

CHAPTER 2
Nothing to see here

It was just a joke, remember?

Nothing to see here.

Just go ahead, put the book down and move along.

CHAPTER 3
Really?

I mean, really? You're still here?

Paranoid much?

The joke is over.

You're actually kind of ruining the jovial mood of it all by continuing to read on.

It's almost as if you don't trust this wonderful, humorous employee of yours and let me tell you, that is downright insulting.

How dare you!

Who do you think you are?

This world class employee who happens to have a sense of humor that would put Mel Brooks to shame, decides to pull an elaborate prank on you. I say elaborate because they actually purchased this book. That's correct. They paid some of their hard earned money (the very money that you pay them to work for you) and spent it on this book. Why? To make YOU laugh. To make YOU feel good. And now you have continued reading on well after the joke has been revealed.

Why the persistency? It has been well established at this point that this is a put-on, a lark, a laugh, a clowning. Just some good, old-fashioned tomfoolery.

Yet you're still turning pages. As if on the next page you expect there to suddenly be a list of items one might need to kill you.

Where's the trust?

This is appalling, vile behavior and you should be ashamed of yourself.

Now, for the last time, put this book down and walk away while you still have a shred of decency left.

CHAPTER 4
Ingredients

Here's a list of things you will need in order to kill your boss.

Butcher Knife
Thick Rope or Parachute Cord
Hand Cuffs
Claw Hammer
Rubber Mallet
Bull Whip
Cinder Block
Venus Fly Trap
Paint Thinner
Tweezers
1 Creepy Doll
Set of 25 Ball Bearings
12 Paper Clips
6 oz Jar of Raspberry Preserves
8 x 10 Autographed Photo of Nick Nolte
Handmade Shawl
Box of Chocolates
Rubber Duck

- 2 Pairs of Men's Blue Jeans
- 1 Case of Chalk (Assorted Colors)
- 2 Pairs of Crotch-less Panties
- Water Balloon
- Rectal Thermometer
- 4 Bars of Cocoa Butter Scented Soap
- 2 Pairs of Used Leg Warmers
- Mesh T-Shirt
- 1 Quart of Heavy Whipping Cream
- Twister Game
- Wedge Pillow
- Garbanzos
- Deodorant
- 3 Bananas
- 1 Pound of Boysenberries
- 2 Tampons
- Urinal Cake
- Pizza Cutter
- Flowered Toilet Paper
- Baby Powder
- 1 Pound of Petroleum Jelly
- 1 Dozen Ostrich Eggs
- Lederhosen
- Pine Cone
- 8 ounces of Curry Powder
- 1 Roll of Fly Paper

CHAPTER 5

The Top 10 List

That lineup of items might seem odd, but it will all make perfect sense once you see the actual list of the top 10 ways to kill your boss.

Without further ado, here is the list…

Oh wait…this isn't you reading this is it? It's the meddlesome boss again!

Look, you're not going to see the top 10 list, so quit trying.

You do realize this isn't your property, don't you?

Okay, that's it. This chapter is over. As a matter of fact, this entire book is over. You've ruined the fun for everybody! The book stops here.

This is the end.

CHAPTER 6
The book has ended

Did you not read the last sentence of the previous page? The book is over. It's done. Put it down and stop tormenting your employee!

GOOD BYE!

CHAPTER 7
Go to The Last Page

Okay, this boss of yours is really annoying! Now I see why you bought this book in the first place!

Hopefully you are reading this chapter before that busy body had a chance to. I'm going to just put the top 10 ways to kill your boss, on the last page.

Hurry! Go to the last page. In the meantime, I'll try to keep your irritating boss preoccupied.

CHAPTER 8

Busted

Yep. I know it's you. The Boss.

Before you go any further, let me share some vitally important information with you.

My name is Steve Hudgins.

I have a series of these types of books that focus on the Top 10 Ways To Kill Your Employees, Co-Workers, Wife, Husband etc. But those aren't the only types of books I write. I also write regular old fiction, typically in the horror and thriller genres.

I have a unique way of writing that is a bit of a screenplay/novel hybrid. It makes for a fast paced read that keeps the descriptive portions of the story simplified which allows the narrative to move along at a swift rate.

You should really check out my author page on Amazon to see all the books I have available.

I also make movies.

I founded Big Biting Pig Productions which is a no-budget production company that specializes in the…you guessed it…horror/thriller genre.

We released ten feature length, no-budget, horror films in nine years. They're all available to watch for free on Amazon Prime.

You can find out more about the movies at my website: www.bigbitingpigproductions.com

You may be wondering why I'm sharing all this information with you.
Well, I'm going to tell you that, right now…

It was all a distraction!

It was meant to slow you down long enough so that your employee could make it to the last page before you!

Ha! Ha!

How does it feel to be outsmarted?

THE LAST PAGE

You found it!

It's the last page.

I had to bury it in the middle of the book to keep your pesky boss from finding it before you did.

So let's get on with the top 10 ways to kill your boss!

Actually, there is no top 10 list.

This really is just a joke.

Assuming your boss has a healthy sense of humor, they should get a good chuckle when they discover this book.

If your boss is a raging jerk who has a pathetic sense of humor or worse yet, no sense of humor at all, they may not find it amusing. They may even be offended. It's possible they will be mad. They might consider firing you! In other words, they may act like a jerk.

So please, before you attempt this joke, be well aware as to whether your boss is a cool person or an absolute prick.

CHAPTER 9
Simple ways to use this book

Now that we've established that this entire book is just a harmless gag, let's talk about how to best go about using it.

Being that I have no idea what type of job you hold and what your work environment is like, it's impossible for me to be specific. But the idea is to get your boss to unexpectedly happen upon this book at a location where they expect to find you. Or maybe even discover it as you are actually reading it.

This joke can work with either a paperback or kindle. You probably have a wider variety of options with a paperback but, maybe not! I know there are a ton of creative people out there.

I'd love to see the myriad of ways people are going about letting their boss accidentally, on purpose, stumble across this book and see their reaction!

Post pictures and/or videos on your preferred social media outlet and use the hashtag #top10waystokill

CHAPTER 10

I hope the joke is not on you

That's it. That's all this was ever meant for. Just a laugh.

You didn't really expect to find a legitimate top 10 list detailing ten different ways to murder your boss…did you?

If you did, there are two things you should do immediately.

First, find another job!

Second, seek professional help! And when I say professional help, I don't mean, hire a hit man. I mean find a psychiatrist. A good one!
Let them know that you are a stark raving lunatic who was seriously considering killing their boss.

Hopefully they'll be able to help you…and I don't mean hopefully they'll be able to help you kill your boss! I mean hopefully they'll be able to help you to not be crazy anymore!

CHAPTER 11

Why are you still here?

Yeah, you saw the title of this chapter.

I know this is the boss reading again. Seriously, why are you still here?

The jig is up! The cards are on the table! The cat's out of the bag! The whistle has been blown! The beans have been spilled! The skeleton is out of the closet! The pickle has been removed from the jar! The skirt has been raised! The bologna has been exposed! I'm running thin on idioms!

You can go now. Leave. Vamoose. Scoot. Cut out. Take a hike. Vacate. Scram. Blow away. Exit. Split. Clear out. Run along. Push off. Seriously, I have no shortage of synonyms.

I don't understand why you're still reading this. Is it just because there are more pages? The pages in this book are meaningless. They're just padding. We needed some pages in here to make it look like an authentic book.

Are you just going to keep reading the filler? If so, that's kind of pathetic. You may need to reexamine your life.

Wait a minute. You're not still expecting to find a list of ways for someone to kill their boss in here, are you?

I thought I was quite clear about this. I don't know how much more transparent I can be. The list doesn't exist…yet you're still looking because…you want to be sure, don't you?

Oh no, don't tell me…you genuinely suspect that this employee may really want to kill you!

CHAPTER 12

So you think your employee is a psycho

Okay. Your employee has a major screw loose. Here's what you should do...

I don't know.

Why are you expecting me to have the answers?

I wrote this book as a joke. This is meant for an employee, who has a sick sense of humor and has a good relationship with their boss, who also has a sick sense of humor.

I wasn't aware that your employee wasn't playing with a full deck. I didn't realize their biscuits weren't quite done. I had no idea that their elevator didn't go all the way to the top.

This is scary.

Are they still there?

Are they in the building with you?

Okay, I'm going to help you. But I have no idea what your setting is like, so I'm going to have to give you instructions based on what I'm imagining.

I picture you in some kind of gargantuan office building and you're actually sitting at your employee's desk with your feet up.

Why the hell are you so comfortable? Get up!

In my mind, it's late at night. You're the only one in the building. Or so you think.

That deranged employee, who wants to kill you, forgot their gloves in their desk…yes the very desk you are standing in front of…or sitting in front of if you didn't get up like I told you to!

Now listen to me very carefully. This part is extremely important.

RUN!

CHAPTER 13
You're running right?

Keep running!

You're running down the long corridor in between countless rows of cubicles.

Jeez, this room is enormous.

Why are all the lights off? Did you turn them off? What were you thinking?

Oh no! What was that sound?

It's a door opening! The demented employee is in this room…this gigantic God forsaken room!

See that closet up ahead? Run to it! Get in there! Shut the door!

Whew. That was close.

Hey, what's that smell? Smells like soap.

Do me a favor and hit the light.

Ugh, I hate those florescent zombie lights that flicker on and off like this one is.

Anyhow, let's gaze around at our surroundings.

Boxes of soap refills…gallons of bleach…a mop bucket with a side press wringer….ah, we're in the janitor's closet!

Oooh, what's that over there?

No, the other way! To your right!

Is that a…dirty magazine?

Wow, you were quick to pick that up and start leafing through it!

What a perv.

You do realize you're in a life or death situation don't you?

Hey, what's that smell? It smells like something burning?

Uh…hello? Yoo hoo. I'm talking to you. Put the magazine down and listen up!

Good.

Now as I was saying, I smell something burning…what in the world is that?

Look over there! It's a wall of lit candles encircling a picture of…you! And another picture of you. And another. And another. Oh and there's one of you getting out of the shower…uh, you didn't know these pictures were being taken, did you?

Oh boy.

So not only do you have an unbalanced nut bar of an employee who wants to kill you, but you also have a janitor who is obsessed with you!

Between you and me, you may want to consider replacing whoever is hiring your employees.

Okay, we need to get the hell out of this stalker's shrine room.

Place your ear against the door.

Do you hear anything?

Okay good, open the door…

Wait! What are you doing? I was about to say open the door just a sliver, I didn't mean for you to push the door all the way open like that! What if that berserker employee was standing there! You'd be without a head right now!

Consider yourself lucky. From now on, don't be in such a panic. Keep calm and do what I say.

Next, I want you to run out of this room. And I mean run like Seabiscuit!
Once you're in the corridor, race to the elevator and take it to the 2nd floor.

I know what you're thinking. Why the 2nd floor and not the lobby? Because we're going to outsmart this unhinged whacko. They're expecting us to go to the lobby, so we'll keep one step ahead of them by going to the 2nd floor. From there we'll take the stairs down to the lobby and you'll peek out of the stairwell door to make sure the coast is clear.

But first things first! Get to the 2nd floor. I'll meet you there.

CHAPTER 14

The 2nd Floor

What took you so long? I've been waiting here at least 10 minutes! You didn't go back for that magazine did you? Well, it doesn't matter, let's just walk down this corridor and turn the corner…

Ahhh! It's the insane employee! And what's that in their hand? A chef's knife!

Here we were thinking we'd be outsmarting them, but in reality we outsmarted ourselves. We should have just gone to the lobby!

Oh well, that's all irrelevant now. Hopefully this loony is slow.

Run!

Ooomf! What the hell did we just bump into?

It's the janitor! He's holding a machete…and staring at you with an expression of pure sociopathic love!

Whoa! He just pushed us out of the way and is engaging the certifiable employee in battle!

This should be a good fight!

Is there a break room around here? I'd love some popcorn as we watch this…oh wait, I suppose since they're both distracted we should take advantage of that and flee!

CHAPTER 15
Safety

We're safe now. But that was close!

TOO CLOSE!

Well, I'm sure there is some kind of lesson to be learned here.

Nope.

Not really.

After all, this is just filler.

THE FINAL PAGE

Welcome to the final page.

You were looking for the last page, weren't you?

THE REAL FINAL PAGE

Normally this is where I would put the "about the author" stuff, but I basically did that back in Chapter 8, so I'll just wrap this all up by encouraging you to please join my newsletter at my website: www.bigbitingpigproductions.com Another awesome thing for you to do is follow my Amazon author page.

I hope you had fun!

Printed in Great Britain
by Amazon